THIS CANDLEWICK BOOK BELONGS TO:

_____

_____

_____

_____

For Josie and Oliver

Copyright © 1995 by Lucy Cousins

All rights reserved.

First U.S. paperback edition 1997

The Library of Congress has cataloged the hardcover edition as follows:

Cousins, Lucy.
Za-Za's baby brother / Lucy Cousins.
Summary: Za-Za the zebra must adjust to the arrival
of a baby brother.
ISBN 1-56402-582-9 (hardcover)
[1. Zebra—Fiction. 2. Babies—Fiction.] I. Title
PZ7.C83175Zaj   1995
[E]—-dc20   94-47190

ISBN 0-7636-0337-6 (paperback)

2 4 6 8 10 9 7 5 3 1

Printed in Hong Kong

This book was typeset in Lucy Cousins.
The pictures were done in gouache.

Candlewick Press
2067 Massachusetts Avenue
Cambridge, Massachusetts 02140

Za-Za's
Baby Brother

Lucy Cousins

CANDLEWICK PRESS
CAMBRIDGE, MASSACHUSETTS

My mom is going to have a baby.

She has a big fat tummy. There's not much room for a hug.

Granny came to
take care of me.

Dad took Mom to the hospital.

When the baby was born we went to see Mom.

When Mom came home she was Very tired. I had to be very quiet and help Dad take care of her.

All my uncles and aunts came to see the baby.

hat a good oy.

Ooh, he's gorgeous.

I played by myself.

Dad was always busy.

Mom was always busy.

"Dad, will you read me a story?"
"Not now, Za-Za. We're going shopping soon."

"Sorry, Za-Za, the baby's hungry and we have to go home."

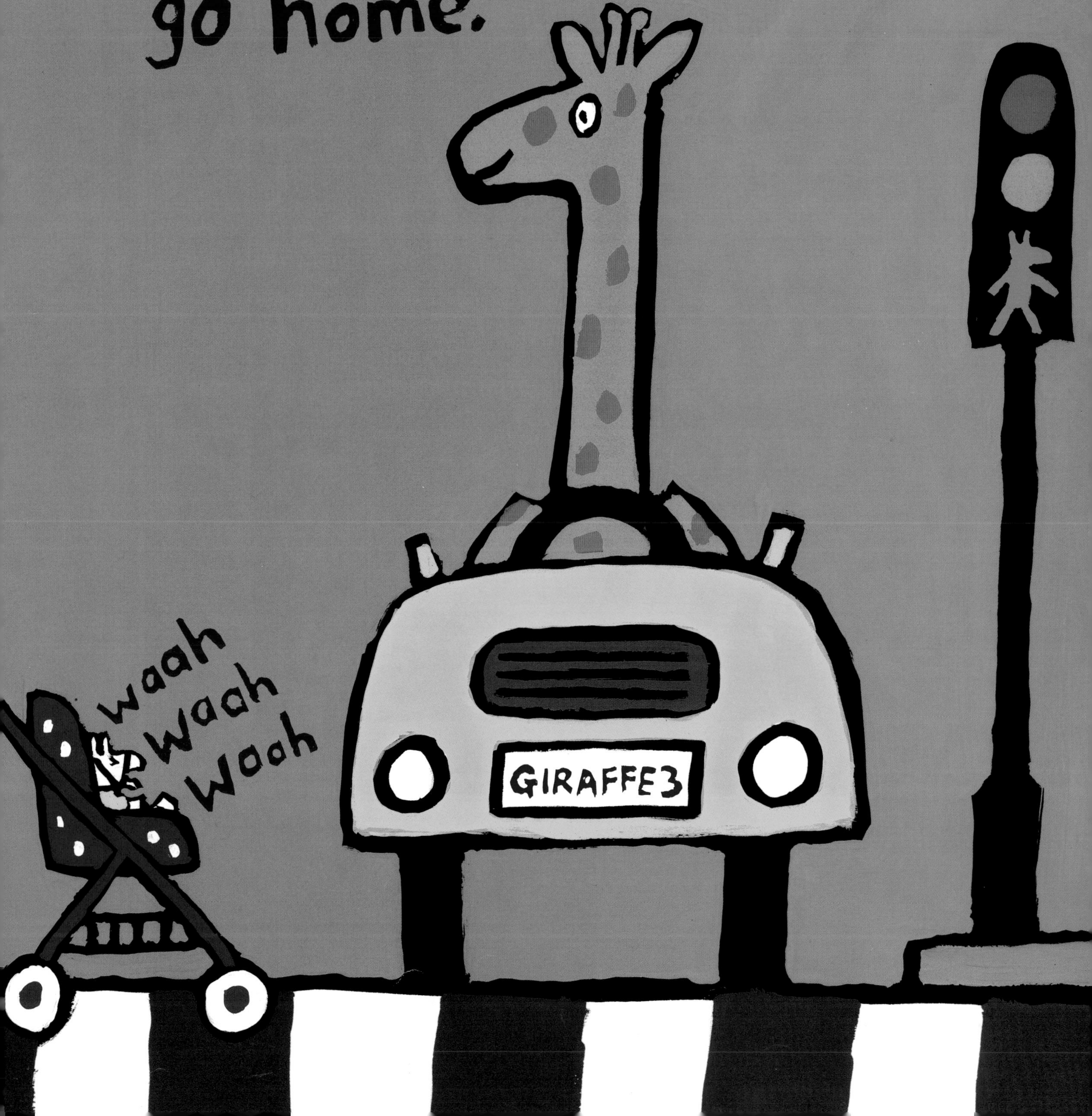

So I hugged the baby...

and I pushed him...

and I built him a tower.

He was nice.
It was fun.

When the baby got tired Mom put him to bed.

Then I got my
hug...

and a bedtime story.